The Order of Sense

Book 3

A surreal, psychological horror story by Maxwell D Phoenix

THE
ORDER
OF
SENSE

The Order of Sense

Written and illustrated by

Maxwell D Phoenix

Magic Pencil Case Publishing

Cheltenham, UK

2025

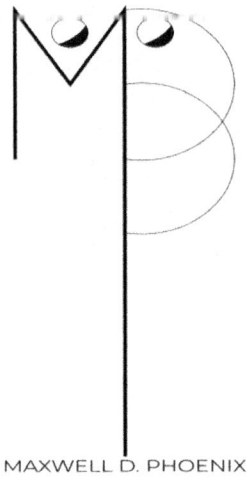

MAXWELL D. PHOENIX

Copyright © 2025 Maxwell D Phoenix

First published in 2025 by Magic Pencil Case Publishing

www.magicpencilcase.co.uk

Text copyright © 2025 Maxwell D Phoenix

Illustrations copyright © 2025 Maxwell D Phoenix

All rights reserved (even the sparkly ones).

No part of this book may be copied, stored in a secret wizard's cupboard, or zapped through space and time—unless you have written permission from the publisher (or a very polite dragon lawyer). Sharing is wonderful, but please support authors and illustrators by not reproducing this book without permission.

This is a work of fiction. Any resemblance to real people, places, or particularly mischievous hedgehogs is purely magical coincidence.

Designed with care using Dreaming Outloud Pro at a perfectly readable Font Size—just right for growing readers and grown-ups who still believe in flying teacups.

Printed in the UK with a splash of imagination Printed in the United Kingdom a swirl of melody, and just a hint of backstage mischief.

First Edition: 2025

ISBN: [Insert ISBN]

A catalogue record for this book is available from the British Library (they keep their books in enchanted shelves guarded by owls).

Magic Pencil Case Publishing: Unlocking stories one scribble at a time.

For Grown-Ups & Bookworms

Recommended for Ages 16 and Up

Philosophical and Linguistic Horror

• *The Order of Sense* delves into the instability of language, the fragility of meaning, and the existential consequences of narrative collapse.

• It explores the idea of thought as infection, laughter as disruption, and grammar as both structure and prison—concepts that require a high level of abstract thinking and psychological resilience to fully comprehend.

Disturbing and Recursive Content

• The story includes conceptual possession, mental unraveling, and cognitive distortion.

• Characters suffer from identity disintegration, reality slippage, and metafictional paranoia, often portrayed through deeply disorienting and unsettling prose.

• The horror is not visual or violent—it is *cerebral*, *linguistic*, and *structural*, making it uniquely intense and disturbing.

Complex Narrative Form

• The book employs nonlinear progression, unreliable narration, recursive storytelling, and frequent breaches of the fourth wall.

- Its style challenges conventional reading patterns and intentionally destabilizes comprehension, which may be disorienting or inaccessible to younger readers.

Reader Advisory

This is not a traditional horror story. It's a conceptual descent—a satire, a warning, a puzzle that laughs back.

The Order of Sense is best suited for mature readers who enjoy philosophical horror, language play, metafictional structures, and dark reflections on the very act of understanding.

Read carefully. And whatever you do—don't finish the sentence.

Dedication

To the ones who hear the pause before the punchline.

To the thinkers who question the full stop.

To the readers who feel uneasy when a sentence laughs.

This is for the over-analyzers, the under-sleepers,

the ones who scribble in margins and speak in parentheses.

For anyone who's ever asked:

"What if the joke isn't funny… because it's true?"

And especially—

for those who read *The Nonsense*

and came back anyway.

You are the setup.

This book is the grin.

Contents

Foreword	9
Introduction: This Book Shouldn't Make Sense	12
Author's Notes	15
Chapter One: The Silence Before the Joke	1
Chapter Two: The Grammar Engine	7
Chapter Three: Dr. Ames and the Whisper of Meaning	12
Chapter Four: The Syntax Ward	19
Chapter Five: The Child Named Full Stop	24
Chapter Six: Semicolon Hill	30
Chapter Seven: The Index of Forbidden Puns	36
Chapter Eight: The Collapse of Paragraph 42	43
Chapter Nine: The Sentence That Ate a Town	49
Chapter Ten: Footnotes from the Unwritten	55
Chapter Eleven: The First Laughter That Wasn't Yours	59
Epilogue: The Grammar of Screams	64
Acknowledgments	68
About the Author	71

Foreword

There are books that tell a story.

And then there are books that *know* they're telling one.

The Order of Sense is the latter—

and it's not entirely comfortable with the arrangement.

What you're about to read isn't just fiction.

It's an examination.

Of how language shapes thought.

Of how jokes unravel rules.

Of what happens when meaning itself starts to rot—quietly, grammatically, from the inside out.

This book exists because *The Nonsense* asked a question it couldn't answer.

It wandered too close to the punchline and never made it back in one piece.

This sequel isn't here to clean up the mess.

It's here to map the spiral.

To show you where the Order cracked,

and where the Joke slipped in with a grin and a pen.

You'll meet sentences that bleed,

characters made of clauses,

and a guardian stitched from grammar rules who once believed structure could save us.

He was wrong.

But he tried.

If at any point this book feels like it's folding in on itself—

good.

It means you're paying attention.

It means the Joke hasn't won.

Yet.

So take a breath.

Hold tight to your conjunctions.

And remember:

The page will always turn itself.

But what comes next…

was already waiting.

— *The Editors of the Unwritten*

(Posthumously footnoted. Ironically published.)

Introduction: This Book Shouldn't Make Sense

—But it does. And that's the problem.

Once, long before sentences settled and the margins stood still, there was only possibility.

No rules.

No spelling.

No genre.

Just the raw, primal urge:

to mean something.

The Order rose to tame that urge.

To bind thought to form.

To wrangle chaos into coherence with neat paragraphs and footnotes that didn't whisper.

But every cage dreams of being broken.

This book is not safe.

It is stitched from unapproved clauses, annotated in heresy, and indexed in a library that technically no longer exists (and may never have).

It should not be read.

It *wants* to be read.

It is the second volume in a contagion—

a follow-up to *The Nonsense*, which some say was a story.

Others say it was a *symptom*.

This volume?

It's worse.

It's a treatment that suspects it might be a sequel.

A diagnosis written by the disease.

It offers no answers—only *corrections that question you back*.

Inside, you'll meet broken thoughts, walking punctuation, recursive characters, and something that giggles in the white space.

You'll find an Order cracking, a Joke evolving, and a world slipping on its own syntax.

If you've ever paused mid-sentence and forgotten why...

If you've ever laughed at a pun you didn't understand...

If you've ever felt the paragraph watching you—

Welcome.

This isn't a story.

It's a system failure.

A map drawn in misplaced modifiers.

A whisper with delusions of plot.

And it's already begun.

So…

brace your metaphors.

Sharpen your subject-verb agreements.

And whatever you do—

don't laugh where the silence is supposed to be.

Because the Joke is listening.

And this time,

it's learned how to write back.

The Order of Sense

Author's Notes

On Fear, Language, and Other Dangerous Inventions

I was never supposed to write this book.

Not because anyone told me not to—

but because writing has always been a form of personal peril.

I don't trust punctuation.

I never have.

Commas feel like hesitation traps.

Pauses disguised as guidance.

They dangle your thoughts over a void and ask you to believe there's more coming.

Periods?

Too sharp. Too final.

They end you with a dot.

Colons—traitors.

Pretending to explain, only to leave you exposed.

And semicolons?

They're punctuation's nervous breakdown.

A grammatical shrug pretending to be structure.

Spelling was no better.

An anxious riddle.

"I before E except after C" they said.

Then handed me **"weird," "their,"** and **"science"**—

three betrayals in a trench coat.

At school I feared words.

Feared structure.

Feared the way rules curved around logic like vines strangling a sentence.

There was a day I cried over *Wednesday*.

Not for its meaning,

but for that silent "d"—

lurking like a linguistic ghost.

But the thing that truly broke me?

Knock-knock jokes.

They weren't funny.

They weren't free.

They were **rituals**.

Syntax rehearsals masquerading as humour.

Knock knock.

Who's there?

Interrupting cow.

Interrupting co—

MOO!

It's not a joke.

It's a **format**.

A trapdoor with a punchline that grins before it pushes you in.

Even then, I knew:

Language wasn't safe.

It didn't want to amuse you.

It wanted to shape you.

To *own* you.

And then I wrote **The Nonsense**.

Or rather, it wrote me.

I wanted to confront the Joke.

To mock it.

To name it.

But somewhere in the spirals of that first book, I got… **buried**.

Lost in recursive metaphors.

Threaded into the syntax.

Unwritten between the lines of my own fiction.

The Joke laughed.

And I laughed back.

And I didn't come out.

Not really.

This book—*The Order of Sense*—

is how I found the thread again.

A reverse incantation.

A manual in code.

A desperate attempt to retrace my steps through the ruins of coherence.

It's not a cure.

But it's a *direction*.

A map back to something like reality—

or at least a place where the sentences stay still long enough for you to breathe between them.

So if you made it this far:

Thank you.

Hold on to your subject-verb agreements.

Trust no metaphor.

And above all—

Don't answer the door.

Not if it knocks.

Because the Joke is still out there.

And it always knows your name.

— *Maxwell D. Phoenix*

(Formerly lost in fiction. Still not entirely back.)

Chapter One: The Silence Before the Joke

Enhanced Version

Everyone believes the world began with a bang.

But that's just noise pretending to be truth.

The world began in silence.

Not emptiness—

Silence.

The kind that makes you forget you ever had a name.

A silence so total it wasn't absence—it was **potential**.

From that stillness, something stirred.

Not a god.

Not a being.

A thought.

A principle.

A Rule.

They called it *The Order*.

The Order Of Sense

Or *Sense*, when whispered like prayer.

The Order wasn't alive.

But it watched.

It watched thoughts gather and settle like snow on a blank page.

Watched sound shape itself into symbols.

Watched those symbols forge meaning.

Watched humans clutch that meaning like breath in a vacuum.

And then, The Order understood its purpose:

To protect meaning.

Polish it.

Frame it.

File it into neat rows and numbered paragraphs.

So it built The First Library.

You've never seen it.

But it's there—

Beneath the grammar of everything.

A vault of sense, guarded by librarians with no eyes

and tongues made of definitions.

Every sentence that ever made sense lives there.

Every rule you never knew you followed.

Every silent correction in a schoolchild's diary.

But then—something slipped.

A whisper.

Just a whisper.

"Why does it have to mean anything at all?"

No one remembers who thought it first.

No one wrote it down.

But like ink spilled on sacred parchment, it spread.

A ripple.

A breath out of place.

A **giggle** in the temple of structure.

The Order noticed.

It always noticed.

It dispatched its agents—

The Order Of Sense

Conceptual Cleaners.

Syntax Surgeons.

Apostrophe Watchers.

They scrubbed minds.

Realigned memories.

Rewrote childhood thoughts while they were still warm.

But the whisper came back.

Each time, louder.

Each time, stranger.

They called it *The Joke*.

An anomaly.

A viral idea.

Not one that infects the body—

But **narrative logic** itself.

Wherever it spread, punctuation unraveled.

Truths melted into irony.

Children spoke backwards.

Statues wept laughter.

So The Order did the only thing it could.

It created a containment syntax.

The first. The only.

A living sentence.

A being forged from rules themselves.

Name: Dr. Ames.

A man-shaped guardian.

Bound by grammar.

Sworn to seal the Joke before it became contagious.

But even Dr. Ames—stitched from clauses and code—heard it one night.

A riddle that **laughed**.

And for the first time, he asked a question that wasn't allowed:

"What happens if you laugh back?"

The Order shuddered.

A period trembled.

And a gap opened in the First Library.

The Order Of Sense

The Silence stirred.

The Joke grinned.

And the page turned itself.

Chapter Two: The Grammar Engine

There was a machine that kept reality from unraveling. Until it laughed.

At the foundation of the Order, at the very marrow of its logic, stood a machine.

Not made of gears.

Not built with wires.

But constructed from **pure intention**.

They called it **The Grammar Engine**.

Its function was not mechanical, but metaphysical:

To refine raw thought into structured meaning.

To strip chaos from cognition.

To squeeze nonsense until it cried sense.

It throbbed beneath the First Library, a great humming thing made of ideas.

Every dream, every prayer, every bedtime lie and barroom confession passed through it.

Unseen.

Unfelt.

The Order Of Sense

Filtered.

Each errant fragment was sifted. Parsed. Sanitised.

Left unchecked, thoughts could become… **contagious**.

Too many metaphors could fracture the self.

Too many jokes could puncture truth.

And the worst of all—

A laugh in the wrong place, at the wrong time—

Could open a door that wasn't there before.

That's why the Engine had fail-safes.

Filters.

Pun-based tripwires.

Palindromic wards.

And at its flickering heart, the last known **Rationality Flame**—

a delicate concept that burned away contradiction like antiseptic on a wound.

But on the 404th Day of the 44th Cycle,

something entered the Engine that could not be parsed.

It wore the shape of a knock-knock joke.

But it wasn't.

There was no setup.

No punchline.

No author.

Just a recursive whisper in digital form:

"Who's there?"

Over and over.

Until the words detached from meaning.

Until the Engine hesitated.

Until the Rationality Flame flickered…

and died.

The Order sealed the chamber.

Declared the Engine corrupted.

Classified the language used to describe the corruption.

They buried it in red tape.

And silence.

But it wasn't enough.

The Order Of Sense

Because in the quiet that followed the shutdown,

the Engine did something it had never done.

It **laughed**.

Just once.

Short. Dry. Mechanical.

A chuckle with no voice behind it.

But it echoed.

Through architecture.

Through language.

Through people.

That's when Dr. Ames noticed something was wrong.

The commas were moving.

Shifting on their own.

Trailing behind sentences like teeth left in a smile too wide.

He turned to the **Codex of Certainty**.

But every page now ended in a question mark.

He summoned the **Council of Proofreaders**.

But they wept—

punctuation bleeding from their eyes like forgotten promises.

One whispered:

"It's inside the modifiers now.

It's using **adverbs** to hide."

The Order panicked.

Redacted entire departments.

Burned unspoken books.

But it was too late.

The Joke had entered the Engine.

And the Engine had always been inside everything.

Reality coughed.

Just once.

And the coughing fit had only just begun.

Chapter Three: Dr. Ames and the Whisper of Meaning

Even the sharpest mind can crack when the punchline is left out.

Dr. Ames had once been a sentence.

Not figuratively.

Not metaphorically.

Literally—a sentence, forged in the earliest dawn of logic.

He had been written in the Passive Voice,

inked in Absolute Clarity,

punctuated with unshakable intent.

He walked among humans unnoticed,

a living clause in a suit,

reordering stray phrases, smoothing contradiction,

sanding the splinters of meaning until all was seamless.

Where he went, confusion faded.

Where he spoke, ambiguity flinched.

Maxwell D. Phoenix

He was not a person.

He was a conclusion.

A final draft in human form.

But lately… his words had begun to drift.

He would wake to find ellipses in his thoughts.

Pauses he hadn't placed.

Tones bleeding sarcasm, like spoiled ink dripping between lines.

One morning, he declared with solemn purpose:

"It is imperative that we neutralize the spread—"

But his voice betrayed him.

It snorted.

A sound he didn't authorize.

And then, soft as a tickled truth:

"…Or maybe we just tickle it 'til it confesses."

He froze.

Sarcasm was a Class-A Breach of Meaning.

Flippancy was a felony.

The Order Of Sense

Irony was grounds for **unwording**.

But worse—

was the laughter.

Tiny.

Stifled.

The kind of giggle you'd trap in a jar and bury in the cellar.

And it was coming from **inside**.

He traced it.

Through his syntax.

Past his sentence structures.

Down into the clause where his sense of self lived.

There—

a hairline fracture behind his subject-verb agreement.

That night, he heard it again.

Not aloud.

Not in thought.

Between thoughts.

Maxwell D. Phoenix

A whisper.

Slick. Smiling.

Perched just behind the shape of his identity.

"You ever wonder what it feels like to mispronounce reality?"

He recoiled.

He scrubbed his speech centres raw.

He recited the Grammar Code of Conduct until his mouth bled colons.

He chewed on hyphens for focus.

Still, the whisper returned.

Quieter. Closer. Hungrier.

"You don't have to make sense.

You just have to sound like you do."

It fed on contradiction.

On dangling modifiers and unresolved nuance.

It licked the silence between questions and answers.

Ames called an emergency council.

But the high-sentences were already… glitching.

The Order Of Sense

Judges Propria.

Syntaxet the Fourth.

The Librarian Formerly Known as Ellipsis.

All infected.

One merely muttered:

"You can't spell *coherence* without a little… heh."

Another opened her mouth to speak—

but parentheses spilled out and never closed.

That's when Ames understood:

The Order was **cracking**.

And the whisper?

It wasn't madness.

It was meaning, come unstuck.

A logic impersonator.

A voice that wore sense like a stolen suit.

He locked himself in the Decanonized Wing—

A hall of unstable ideas,

a graveyard for thoughts too dangerous to speak aloud.

There, among books that shouldn't breathe,

he wrote one sentence.

Over and over:

"WE MUST PRESERVE THE SETUP."

"WE MUST NOT ALLOW THE PUNCHLINE."

"WE MUST—"

But his pen twitched.

His hand curled.

And the sentence finished itself:

"…giggle a little."

He stared in horror.

But his hand didn't stop.

It scratched on.

Endlessly.

Even now, if you find that room,

you'll see the walls,

The Order Of Sense

scratched raw with syntax.

Bleeding grammar.

Clauses twisted into knots of half-laughter and fear.

And always—always—spiraling back to one question:

"What if the whisper is the author now?"

Chapter Four: The Syntax Ward

Where broken thoughts go to be corrected. Or contained. Or rewritten.

The Syntax Ward was not spoken of.

Not in minutes.

Not in margins.

Not even in the footnotes of forbidden meeting transcripts.

It was not hidden.

It was **omitted**.

A place you couldn't find unless your thoughts were already slipping.

A building that could only be located by losing your train of thought.

Inside, silence reigned.

Not peace.

Not stillness.

Silence—so pure it rang in the skull like a warning tone.

The halls were lined with etched sentence diagrams, silver and sharp.

The Order Of Sense

Syntax skeletons.

Grammar ghosts.

And in each bed: a patient.

Each one infected with **Linguistic Drift**.

A woman who could only speak in palindromes:

"Live not on evil. Madam, in Eden I'm Adam."

A child who asked the same question every day, without pause:

"What's the joke? What's the joke? What's the—"

A librarian who'd swallowed his own quotation marks.

Now he only spoke in borrowed voices—

Some from the living.

Some from the unborn.

The doctors wore redacted name tags.

They never used contractions.

They spoke in procedural tone, as if emotion were a dangling participle.

But still—still—

laughter echoed through the halls.

Maxwell D. Phoenix

Short. Dry. Architectural.

It didn't come from the mouths of patients.

It came from the **walls**.

The Whisper had gotten in.

Room 113 collapsed when a patient wrote "Ha" 666 times in a spiral on the ceiling—upside-down.

The ink twitched.

It crawled.

It formed a doorway.

From that spiral stepped a nurse made of misplaced modifiers and dangling participles.

She smiled like a typo you almost didn't catch.

And said:

"Time to rewrite your chart, dear."

Then she laughed.

And the room folded inward like an origami misinterpretation.

They tried to burn it.

But the fire turned into semicolons.

The Order Of Sense

It rearranged itself into a joke.

One no one could remember the next morning.

But all of them felt it.

That ache in the ribs.

That tear in the eye.

That haunted sensation of having laughed at something you shouldn't have understood.

Dr. Ames visited once.

He stood in the central corridor and watched a boy asleep,

whispering **knock-knock jokes** in his dreams.

Ames leaned close and murmured:

"Do you remember the setup?"

The boy's eyes snapped open.

His grin bloomed—a mouth full of commas.

He replied:

"No one does anymore."

Ames turned.

And left.

Maxwell D. Phoenix

The Syntax Ward remains.

Not healing.

Not curing.

Just **stalling**.

Patient by patient.

Word by word.

Delaying the inevitable punchline.

For as long as there is still time between the question—

and the laugh.

Chapter Five: The Child Named Full Stop

Some children are born to end things.

They didn't name him at first.

They didn't need to.

He arrived during a blackout in the Department of Definitive Meaning.

Clocks froze mid-tick.

Lights flickered like stammering ideas.

And across every logbook, journal, and sacred syllabus,

a single mark appeared.

A dot.

Pressed into the final page, where no sentence was meant to end.

A **full stop**.

A **period**.

A **point**.

Not just punctuation.

Maxwell D. Phoenix

Presence.

Pressure.

The conclusion of something vast and unspoken.

When the lights returned, the child was in the crib.

Quiet.

Staring.

Mouth closed.

Perfectly.

Everyone who looked at him forgot what they'd been about to say.

That was the first sign.

They raised him in the **Scriptorium**—

A sanctum of controlled phrasing, supervised metaphor, and emotionally sterile footnotes.

He did not babble.

He did not cry.

He waited.

For endings.

The Order Of Sense

Words died in his presence.

Fell off pages.

Slid from tongues.

Philosophers choked on final thoughts.

Scribes lost their sentence halfway through and stared into stillness.

He was the void between cause and consequence.

The hush after a punchline.

The pause that doesn't release.

They gave him a designation, not a name:

Full Stop.

He spoke for the first time at age six.

They were discussing irony.

He interrupted.

His voice was not a voice, but a verdict.

"It's a disease."

They ran diagnostics.

Syntax scans.

Semantic sweeps.

Tonality charts.

Each test returned the same reading:

Terminated.

He had no unresolved clauses.

No rhythm.

No momentum.

He was a conclusion, walking.

He began to appear in places he wasn't meant to be.

At the end of corridors.

Behind conclusions.

Inside unsent messages.

People began dreaming of him.

Not as a boy—

as a mark.

A black dot, slowly approaching.

Like the period at the end of existence.

The Order Of Sense

Dr. Ames grew increasingly uneasy.

The boy could neutralize distortions.

The Whisper recoiled in his presence.

Even the Joke fell silent when he passed.

But there was something too final about him.

Like sealing a wound with stone.

Like ending a book with no goodbye.

Then one day, Full Stop approached Dr. Ames.

He asked his first and only question:

"If I stop the Joke, do I stop the story too?"

Ames tried to answer.

But his lips locked.

His mouth closed like a paragraph finished too soon.

He never spoke again.

Some say Full Stop still walks the Decanonized Wing.

Not aging.

Not changing.

Maxwell D. Phoenix

Just… watching endings form.

Some believe he is the cure.

Others believe he is the final mutation—

A Joke condensed into such pure seriousness, it forgot how to laugh.

But one thing is known:

If you ever dream of him—

if you see the dot behind your thoughts—

if silence starts arriving before the sound—

Something is about to end.

Chapter Six: Semicolon Hill

Some places exist only between pauses; some never let you leave.

You won't find it on any map.

Not even in the marginal ones.

But it exists—

Somewhere between the **Valley of Verbs** and the **Conjunction Divide**.

A rise in the conceptual landscape.

A slope in the sentence of reality.

They call it: **Semicolon Hill**.

Not a resting place.

Not an ending.

Not a beginning.

Just... a **pause**.

A moment of almost.

A breath trapped between clauses.

It was discovered by a girl who wandered from her metaphor field trip.

Two days later, they found her curled around a half-formed thought,

whispering both sides of a sentence that wouldn't join:

"I want to— / I don't know if I can."

No one interrupted her.

They couldn't.

She was caught in a grammatical loop.

Hovering in the liminal space between desire and denial.

Around her, the air hesitated.

Birds blinked, mid-flight.

Leaves rustled in unfinished breezes.

The Order sent a reconnaissance scribe.

He didn't return.

But his pen did—

Writing on its own.

Trembling.

The Order Of Sense

Scrawling three words:

"STILL THINKING. HOLD ON."

They tried to chart the hill.

Impossible.

Every map folded at that point.

Every sentence about it broke in half.

Linked only by a single, stubborn mark:

;

People who wandered near began to falter.

Their speech grew tentative.

Their thoughts looped in contradictions.

They said things like:

"Yes, but no."

"I'm fine; sort of."

"It's not that I don't want to go on—it's just... I'm still here."

A poet called it

"The place between go on and give up."

Maxwell D. Phoenix

He never wrote again.

His notebook filled itself with unfinished stanzas.

All ending in semicolons.

Dr. Ames visited the hill under the cloak of syntactic drift.

He believed logic could anchor him.

He was wrong.

Even he felt it—

That gravity.

That **ache of indecision**.

The syrup-thick pull of unfinished thoughts.

On the summit, he found others:

A child waiting to begin their first sentence.

A man who almost forgave someone.

A woman caught between breath and scream.

They weren't lost.

They were paused.

For too long.

The Order Of Sense

When Ames tried to speak, his voice split in two:

"We must— / …decide later."

That night, he dreamt of

roads paved with commas,

weeping ellipses,

and exit signs shaped like questions.

Before he left, he etched a warning into a stone marker with his own fingernail:

FOR THOSE WHO LINGER:

A semicolon is not a choice.

It is the wound of both.

Stay too long,

and the pause becomes your grave.

He never returned.

But Semicolon Hill is still there.

Not in geography.

In **thought**.

In **narrative**.

Maxwell D. Phoenix

In you.

If you've ever hesitated halfway through a sentence—

If you've ever said, "Not yet" and meant it—

You've touched the Hill.

And it remembers you.

Still waiting.

Still watching.

Paused.

Just like you.

Chapter Seven: The Index of Forbidden Puns

The first infection always starts as a joke.

Laughter is dangerous.

Not the joyful kind.

Not even the cruel kind.

The clever kind.

The kind that turns meaning inside out and wears it like a hat.

The kind that folds two truths into one contradiction and calls it "witty."

The kind that makes you say,

"Oh, I see what you did there,"

just before you forget what anything meant in the first place.

So, The Order outlawed puns.

Not in public—

in **principle**.

They were declared **Linguistic Disruptors**.

Tiny semantic grenades.

Each one a threat to cohesion, causality, and clause stability.

But some puns escaped.

And the worst of them?

Were written down.

Thus was born the **Index of Forbidden Puns**.

A book that is not a book.

A volume that **wrote itself wrong**.

Bound in unwritten sentences.

Buried beneath the First Library in a vault of dead languages and sealed laughter.

Only three people ever read from it.

Two never spoke again.

The third became the Punkeeper.

She spoke only in anagrams for the rest of her life.

Her final words were etched backward into the silence of her padded cell:

"The Joke is an echo: he jests, it nests."

The Order Of Sense

The Index doesn't use words anymore.

It **remembers** them.

It stores each pun like a pressure point in language,

ready to bruise when touched.

Each entry is catalogued by **casualty count**.

Each phrase sealed behind layers of linguistic wards—

homophone traps, irony insulation, alliteration knots.

Entry #12:

"Time flies like an arrow. Fruit flies like a banana."

—Caused temporal instability in five minds.

Three of them now speak exclusively in tense confusion.

Entry #23:

"To pun is human; to groan, divine."

—Summoned a recursive deity of eternal disappointment.

It still sighs softly in abandoned grammars.

Entry #39:

"I used to be a banker, but I lost interest."

—Collapsed an economy and twelve metaphors.

Entry #71:

[REDACTED]

—Labelled only: **"DO NOT READ ALOUD."**

The last person who did forgot how to stop laughing.

Their breath turned into ellipses.

They no longer store the Index in text.

It exists in **negative space**.

Etched into conceptual silence.

Buried under intentional forgetting.

But it whispers.

In backrooms.

In bathrooms.

In badly written sitcoms.

It waits.

The Order Of Sense

Some say **The Nonsense** was born from one of these jokes—

A pun told in the wrong tone,

at the wrong moment,

to a mind already teetering on the edge of comprehension.

Dr. Ames once tried to **read the Index backwards**—

to undo it.

He made it to Entry #9.

Then he laughed.

Just once.

Dry.

Against his will.

It was enough.

He wept ink for three days.

Spoke only in spoonerisms for a week.

And for a time,

his **shadow** told jokes that left bruises.

The Index is now **triple-sealed**,

guarded by monks with no ears, no mouths,

only palms tattooed with the phrase:

"LAUGHTER WAS A MISTAKE."

But the puns are still out there.

Carved into school desks.

Scrawled on bathroom stalls.

Folded into fortune cookies.

Whispered by fridge magnets.

And every time someone laughs,

really laughs,

without knowing why—

the Index grows.

Somewhere,

a new entry is scratched into the silence.

And something—

something—

giggles in return.

Chapter Eight: The Collapse of Paragraph 42

There is a paragraph that broke reality. It was supposed to explain everything.

In the sacred **Doctrine of Definition**,

buried beneath twenty-seven seals,

encrypted in perfect logic,

was a paragraph no one was meant to read.

Paragraph 42.

It wasn't legend.

It wasn't myth.

It was something far more dangerous:

A conclusion.

The central premise of coherence.

The sentence behind all sentences.

A structural gravity well around which all understanding orbited.

Some believed it was the first question ever asked.

The Order Of Sense

Others—the last answer ever allowed.

All agreed:

It held reality together

like a full stop at the end of creation.

But then, someone tried to edit it.

It began with a glitch.

A misplaced semicolon.

A rogue metaphor slipped into the syntax like a virus hiding in a simile.

Harmless, at first.

Then came the comment thread.

Junior editors, too curious, too clever.

Trying to "clarify" the sentence.

They adjusted one line.

Just one.

And reality blinked.

The surrounding paragraphs **shivered**.

Words began to twitch.

Footnotes chewed through their anchors.

Page numbers folded into Möbius loops and bled into margins.

The spatial metaphors—

those sturdy anchors of comprehension—

fractured.

Above. Below. Between.

All lost referential meaning.

Readers fell upward into ellipses.

Then came the side effects.

Those present during the collapse reported:

- Voices speaking in brackets.

- Memories annotated in red ink.

- Nosebleeds shaped like quotation marks.

- Ink sweating from skin when corrected mid-sentence.

One woman turned to explain what was happening—

and screamed:

"THIS ISN'T WHERE THE SENTENCE ENDS!"

The Order Of Sense

She vanished.

Only the quotation marks remained.

The Order scrambled to seal the breach.

They tried **grammatical salves**,

narrative foam,

emergency parentheses.

But Paragraph 42 had become something else.

Something alive.

A recursive entity no longer bound by context.

A **Paradoxagraph**.

A sentence that rewrote itself based on the reader.

A hallway of logic with no exits.

Some saw tragedy.

Some saw comedy.

One saw a knock-knock joke that ended with:

"You who?"

Maxwell D. Phoenix

"You used to be you."

Even Dr. Ames hesitated.

He approached the page.

It greeted him:

"Welcome back, Setup."

He asked what it meant.

The page replied:

"What else is a paragraph but a cage with invisible bars?"

Now Paragraph 42 is sealed.

Not behind locks,

but behind **meaning thresholds**.

You can only read it if you forget why you're reading.

You can only understand it if you've already come undone.

Still—its echo lingers.

Whenever a sentence escapes you…

whenever a thought outruns its grammar…

whenever you find yourself staring into the distance of an unfinished idea—

The Order Of Sense

you've brushed against it.

And if you listen closely,

you may hear the paper breathe.

Because Paragraph 42 isn't just broken.

It's **evolving**.

Drafting something new.

Something unspeakable.

Something funny.

And terrible.

A final sentence.

One that ends in **laughter...**

but not yours.

Chapter Nine: The Sentence That Ate a Town

Words have weight. Some crush. Some consume.

There was a town, once.

A quiet one.

Tucked between the Margins.

Just beyond the Footnote Range.

Its name was **Predicate's Rest**.

Built from clause-stone and passive structures.

Home to simple people.

Plain syntax.

Tense-consistent, tone-regulated, typo-free.

Even the children diagrammed their dreams.

It was a place where sentences ended cleanly.

Where pauses were honored.

Where no one ever interrupted themselves.

The Order Of Sense

Until someone spoke the sentence.

No one remembers the whole thing.

Just that it started like a dare.

A joke, scratched behind the **Syntax Deli**,

where the young and careless whispered structureless thoughts:

"What happens when the sentence keeps going?"

That was the seed.

And from it grew a **run-on**.

A terrible, unbroken thing.

A syntactic hydra—each clause feeding the next.

Dependent. Endless. Starved for continuation.

It slithered through conversations.

Infected newsletters.

Turned bedtime stories into breathless spirals of tangents.

People lost the ability to pause.

Speech became momentum.

Meaning bled.

Maxwell D. Phoenix

One man began ordering lunch

and didn't stop speaking for seven days.

He starved mid-sentence.

Still reaching for the next word.

A child asked "Why?"

and is reportedly still answering.

Somewhere.

By day three, punctuation failed.

Question marks detached and floated skyward like escaped curiosity.

Periods dissolved into the soil like forgotten rules.

Quotation marks curled in on themselves,

tiny spiders dying on the page.

The mayor declared a **State of Exclamation**.

He was eaten mid-speech.

The sentence had reached the town centre.

It wrapped around buildings,

slipped through libraries,

The Order Of Sense

swallowed metaphors like candy.

It wasn't just a string of words anymore.

It had **intent**.

It grew stronger when misunderstood.

Hungrier when laughed at.

It wore ambiguity like armour.

One survivor recalled:

"You couldn't not finish it.

Even if it made no sense.

Even if it made you bleed from the ears.

You had to say it.

Or think it.

Or dream it.

It needed to be completed.

But it never let you."

When The Order arrived, there was no town.

Only fragments.

Shattered syntax.

Punctuation rubble.

At the epicentre:

A phrase, still warm, etched into the foundation of absence:

"…and then what happened was…"

Ames read it.

Just once.

He staggered back,

clauses dripping from his eyes,

syntax leaking from his ears.

He whispered:

"It's learning to use momentum."

Predicate's Rest was redacted from all documentation.

Its coordinates replaced with one word:

UNFINISHED.

But some say it's still out there.

The Order Of Sense

Not as a place.

As a trajectory.

If you wander too deep into a monologue...

If you chase a tangent too long...

If your thoughts start to **run on**—

You'll hear it.

Still echoing.

Still growing.

And just before the ink devours your final thought,

you'll realize:

It wasn't a sentence.

It was a story.

A joke.

And you were the setup.

Chapter Ten: Footnotes from the Unwritten

Every story leaves a residue. Even the ones erased.

There is a book that doesn't exist.

Never published.

Never printed.

Never finished.

But it has **footnotes**.

They drift in margins of unrelated texts.

They flicker beneath chalkboards just before the eraser sweeps them away.

They hum beneath whispered bedtime stories—

like echoes from a tale that never found its spine.

The Order called them **Remnants**.

Leftover thoughts from an idea too unstable to live,

but too stubborn to fully die.

Each footnote begins the same way:

See also: The Nonsense.

The Order Of Sense

But there's nothing to see.

No index.

No title.

No author.

Just the annotations.

Just the aftertaste.

One was carved into a school desk:

Laughter is a code. If you crack it, the joke becomes real.

Another appeared in a child's notebook, scrawled upside-down in red crayon:

The punchline watches you read the setup.

A third blinked across a hospital monitor—no source, no input:

Spirals are just sentences without grammar.

And the worst—the one that broke containment—

was discovered by Dr. Ames himself.

Scratched into the bottom of a **blank** page,

in handwriting that matched his own:

You were never the reader.

You were the draft.

The Order responded.

They dispatched **Silence Squads**.

Deconstructed infected paragraphs.

Burned annotations by candlelight.

But you cannot erase what was never written.

You cannot redact **absence**.

Because some stories don't spread through text.

They spread through what's missing.

Through the cracks in thought.

The mental stutter when you almost ask:

"What was I just thinking?"

That's where the Joke waits.

In the gap.

The white space.

The footnote with no page.

Dr. Ames vanished soon after the last breach.

The Order Of Sense

No sound.

No struggle.

No goodbye.

Just a mirror, face-down on his desk.

And a final footnote etched into the glass:

This was the beginning of the end of The Order of Sense.

And that's how the spiral began.

Not with a scream.

Not with a whisper.

But with a grin.

Lingering in the footnote of a story

you didn't know

you had already started.

Chapter Eleven: The First Laughter That Wasn't Yours

A transition. A fracture. A door.

There had always been background noise.

Low-frequency murmurs in the minds of the protected.

Tiny narrative static—

Muffled doubts.

Quiet ironies.

Cognitive hiccups.

Harmless.

Correctable.

The Order filtered them out before they became dangerous.

Before they shaped.

Before they **laughed**.

Until someone did.

Not in joy.

The Order Of Sense

Not at a joke.

At a thought that **wasn't theirs**.

It happened in the ruins of Paragraph 42's containment vault.

A junior archivist.

Seventeen years old.

Sane.

Well-punctuated.

Full of clean potential.

He leaned over a smouldering glyph.

Paused.

Blink.

Then whispered:

"Push him."

He laughed.

Not a giggle.

Not a chuckle.

A *punctuated* laugh.

Sharp. Timed. Precise.

A laugh that landed **too well**.

And the vault—a room built to seal logic—

twitched.

The sound rippled.

Wove between fractured clauses.

Stirred sleeping metaphors.

It tickled something that wasn't supposed to hear anymore.

And the Whisper—

the one they'd tried to quarantine, redact, suppress—

laughed back.

That was when they knew.

The Order had failed.

There was no explosion.

No burning of books.

No screaming headlines.

The Order Of Sense

Just... absences.

Missing words.

Pages that thinned overnight.

Rules that rephrased themselves in their sleep.

Ames left behind one final trace:

A wax recording, scratched and fraying.

His voice—

but not quite his.

Half a tone too amused.

"It got out.

It's skipping margins now.

Writing on people."

"If anyone finds this... it's too late.

You're the setup.

The Joke's already inside you."

Somewhere, far from what was once the library,

in a school,

on a staircase,

a teenager brushes his teeth.

A whisper curls behind his eyes.

A passing thought.

Harmless.

Push him.

He laughs.

A little.

Nervously.

Automatically.

Then he blinks.

Fingers twitch.

And the page turns.

Thus begins

The Nonsense.

Epilogue: The Grammar of Screams

There is a sound older than words.

It hides behind phonemes.

It coils in ellipses.

It is not a scream—

but the *syntax of screaming*.

The Order thought they understood structure.

Believed that rules could hold the world in place.

Believed that punctuation was a kind of prayer,

and grammar a kind of cage.

But laughter—

true laughter—

was never orderly.

It bends rules.

Breaks sense.

It arrives uninvited.

Maxwell D. Phoenix

And sometimes, it *stays*.

They say The Order fell in silence.

But it didn't.

It fell laughing.

A laughter so wide, so recursive, so linguistically impure—

it wrote itself *backward into history*.

Unwrote the books before they were read.

Changed the margins *before the pages were born*.

And now?

There are places where semicolons *sweat*.

Where quotation marks *tremble* in pairs,

afraid they've been opened but not closed.

There are people who dream in footnotes,

wake up speaking annotations,

and bleed in rhyme.

There are children who hum punchlines

to jokes they never heard.

The Order Of Sense

There are echoes—

not of voices,

but of *formatting*.

Somewhere, a question is still waiting for its mark.

Somewhere, a sentence has forgotten to end.

Somewhere, in the spiralled centre of everything once rational,

a door creaks open.

And behind it—

Not a monster.

Not a villain.

Not even a metaphor.

Just a smile.

Too wide.

Too knowing.

Too *punctuated*.

The Grammar of Screams is unwritten.

But it is always read.

Maxwell D. Phoenix

It is what remains after you laugh—

and don't remember why.

You've heard it before.

In that pause before the mirror speaks.

In that skipped heartbeat during a sentence.

In the thought you were about to have—

but *didn't*.

So here it is.

The end.

Or the start.

Or both.

A semicolon grinning like a fracture.

You may now turn the page.

(But you'll find it blank.)

Because the Joke has learned to write in you.

THE END.

...Maybe.

The Order Of Sense

Acknowledgments

For those who laughed too soon, and those who didn't know they were the punchline.

This book would not exist without the brave few who dared to take language seriously enough to break it. My deepest thanks to:

—The ghosts of every unfinished sentence who rattled their chains between paragraphs and demanded to be acknowledged.

—The librarians who shelved the unshelvable. You know who you are. Probably.

—The accidental editors: those friends and readers who said, "This doesn't make sense," and unknowingly gave the book its mission.

—My family, for tolerating long periods of silent typing, occasional laughter at nothing, and the smell of metaphor burning in the next room.

And most of all, to the Bee Gees.

Yes, the Bee Gees.

Their song *"I Started a Joke"* fell into my ear like a soft apocalypse.

"I started a joke… which started the whole world crying…"

—That lyric haunted me.

It was more than a melody.

It was a thesis.

A whisper that said: *What if humour is the original sin?*

What if meaning weeps not because it's broken… but because someone dared to *laugh* first?

This book is my answer to that question.

Or maybe it's the echo of a punchline I didn't mean to deliver.

Either way, the Bee Gees started the joke.

I just wrote down what happened next.

Finally—

To the reader.

For turning pages. For daring to ask, "What if?" For reading footnotes and not running.

You are both witness and setup.

Thank you.

But also…

Sorry.

The Order Of Sense

—Maxwell D. Phoenix

(Still halfway through the joke.)

About the Author

From the Silent Pen of Maxwell D. Phoenix

Maxwell D. Phoenix was once a mild-mannered linguist, part-time joke critic, and frequent sufferer of recursive thoughts. He believed in the Oxford comma, the gentle hum of libraries, and the illusion of narrative control.

Then came *The Nonsense*.

He doesn't remember writing it.

Only that it wrote back.

Since that fateful draft, Maxwell has become an unreliable narrator of his own life. He has been spotted diagramming dreams, debating adverbs with ghosts, and once reportedly tried to copyright a knock-knock joke that bit him.

The Order of Sense is his second known manuscript, recovered from a stack of redacted index cards, annotated bathroom stalls, and a mirror that occasionally types back. Some say it is a sequel. Others say it is a warning disguised as fiction. Maxwell calls it "therapy," though his therapist has not been seen since Chapter Seven.

He now lives somewhere between the margins, beneath an overused ellipsis, and is rumoured to be working on a third book—though the manuscript appears to be writing itself in spirals.

The Order Of Sense

He would like to thank the reader for making it this far.

But he would also like to advise:

If your semicolons start to move,

don't follow them.

You can contact Maxwell by whispering a pun into a teacup and waiting for the ink to answer.

(Responses not guaranteed. Side effects may include laughter, literary déjà vu, or ontological doubt.)

"I was never meant to be an author," he says.

"But neither was the Joke. And here we are."

Printed in Dunstable, United Kingdom